# Farmer Joe Goes to the City

by **Nancy Wilcox Richards**

illustrated by
**Werner Zimmermann**

Scholastic Canada Ltd.
Toronto  New York  London  Auckland  Sydney
Mexico City  New Delhi  Hong Kong  Buenos Aires

*For my two-year-old daughter, Jennifer Elyse,*
*who already loves to go shopping.*
*– N. W. R.*


*To Petra,*
*her patience and her computer.*
*– W. Z.*

Scholastic Canada Ltd.
604 King Street West, Toronto, Ontario M5V 1E1, Canada

Scholastic Inc.
557 Broadway, New York, NY 10012, USA

Scholastic Australia Pty Limited
PO Box 579, Gosford, NSW 2250, Australia

Scholastic New Zealand Limited
Private Bag 94407, Botany, Manukau 2163, New Zealand

Scholastic Children's Books
Euston House, 24 Eversholt Street, London NW1 1DB, UK

The illustrations were painted in watercolours on Arches paper.

Library and Archives Canada Cataloguing in Publication
Richards, Nancy Wilcox, 1958-
Farmer Joe goes to the city / by Nancy Wilcox Richards ; illustrations by Werner Zimmermann.
ISBN 978-1-4431-1376-2
I. Zimmermann, H. Werner (Heinz Werner), 1951- II. Title.
PS8585.I184F2 2012          jC813'.54          C2011-908100-8

6 5 4 3 2 1     Printed in Singapore 46     12 13 14 15 16

Farmer Joe lived with his wife
in an old house
in the middle of a big field.

1

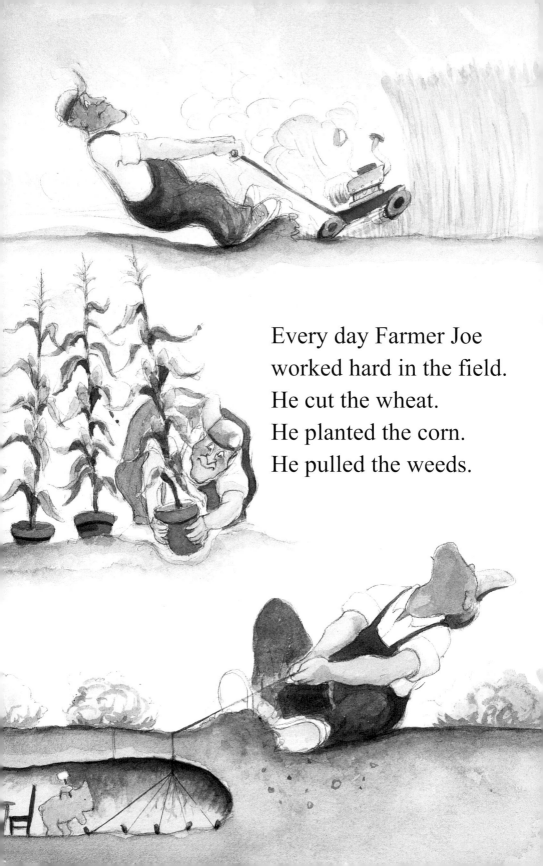

Every day Farmer Joe
worked hard in the field.
He cut the wheat.
He planted the corn.
He pulled the weeds.

But one day he said to himself,
"Tomorrow is my wife's birthday.
I will go to the city and buy her
a present. Something special."

Bumpity-bump-bump-bump
went the truck over the dirt roads.

Clangity-clang-clang-clang
into the busy city.

Farmer Joe was puzzled. There were so many stores! "I need to find something special," he said to himself. "And red, because that's her favourite colour."

7

Cars whizzed this way and that.
Buses zoomed here and there.
Trucks sped up one street
and down another.

Then Farmer Joe saw a big store. A very
big store. It was the biggest store he'd
ever seen. Farmer Joe parked his truck
and went in.

Inside were even more stores.
Shoppers whizzed this way
and that. Escalators zoomed
here and there. Elevators sped
up one floor and down another.

Farmer Joe came to a grocery store.
He picked up a big juicy apple. "It's
red," he thought, "but not very special."

At the next store, he looked at some
shiny red boots. "Not special enough,"
he said.

Farmer Joe went into a clothing store.
Inside he saw some warm underwear.
"These are very red," he said.
"But still not special enough."

Farmer Joe was very sad.
He had whizzed this way and that.
He had zoomed here and there.
He had sped from one store to another.
And he still hadn't found a present
for his wife.

Then Farmer Joe spotted a sign.
It was a red sign.
And it was above a big red store.

Farmer Joe went into the store.

"I'm looking for something red,"
he told the man behind the counter.

"Something special?" asked the salesman.

"Yes!" said Farmer Joe. "Very special."

"How about this?" asked the salesman.

Farmer Joe looked. It was
very red. And he knew right
away that it was very, very
special. "Perfect!" he said.

Farmer Joe drove back to his old house
in the middle of his big field.
Past the cars whizzing this way and that.
Past the buses zooming here and there.
Past the trucks speeding up one street
and down another.

Farmer Joe woke up very early
the next morning. He cooked a special
breakfast for his wife. On the table was
the very special present.

Later, Farmer Joe
went out to his field.
He cut the wheat.
He planted the corn.
He pulled the weeds.
He was very happy.

And so was his wife!